American Horse Tales

Hollywood

by Samantha M. Clark

Penguin Workshop

For the horse lovers in my family and everywhere—SMC

PENGUIN WORKSHOP
An imprint of Penguin Random House LLC, New York

First published in the United States of America by Penguin Workshop,
an imprint of Penguin Random House LLC, New York, 2021

Copyright © 2021 by Penguin Random House LLC

Visit us online at penguinrandomhouse.com.

Library of Congress Control Number: 2021932448

Printed in the United States of America

ISBN 9780593225271   10 9 8 7 6 5 4 3 2 1

Chapter 1
The Big Chance

Juniper gripped the reins tighter as her horse sped across the paddock. Balancing carefully, she pulled her right leg up and over her horse's back. She crouched on the stirrup at his side, and when her target was near, Juniper thrust out her arm.

"Take that, fire breath!" she shouted, brandishing her makeshift sword in the air. "We got it, Able. We got the dragon!"

As the horse sped away, Juniper pushed up onto

Able's back again. She flipped around so she was sitting backward, then grinned at the massive elm tree they had just passed, its crooked branches like clawed arms reaching out to catch them.

Juniper patted her horse's side as he slowed to a trot. "If that really was a dragon, Able, we could've taken it. You and me—we're the best team ever, right?"

She peered over her shoulder as Able neighed, nodding his head as though he agreed wholeheartedly.

Juniper spun around to face forward and said, "Let's go again. This time, let's circle around, like Lady Penelope does on *Castle McAvoy*."

Able's ears twitched as Juniper hunched over his neck, then the horse took off.

"Woo-hoo!" Juniper shouted. "Watch out, all ye drag—"

The rest of her war cry got stuck in her throat. A figure over by the stables caught her eye. It was someone who wasn't supposed to be there. Someone who had said he'd be working in his office for at least the next hour.

Juniper quickly pulled back on Able's reins.

"Abort! Abort!" she said, steering the horse toward the stable. With a nervous laugh, she whispered, "The *real* dragon is watching us now."

Juniper's father shook his head as they trotted toward him.

"What are you still doing in the paddock?" Her father took hold of Able's reins while Juniper slid from her horse's back. "Able's supposed to be cleaned, fed, and resting by now."

"I was going to . . . ," Juniper began, trying to think of an answer that didn't include swords or dragons, but nothing came to her mind.

Her father brushed dust off Able's side. "You can't clean him from the saddle, you know." His eyes dropped to Juniper's waist, then narrowed. "And why is the rasp tucked into your belt?"

Oops! Juniper looked down and yanked the rasp out from where she had secured it tightly between her belt and her jeans. She waved it in the air like she was using it to attack an enemy. "It was my sword?" Each word was filled with uncertainty, as though it wanted to run back into her mouth and hide.

"Wait, don't tell me: A troll is on the grounds, and you just *had* to protect the ranch." Her dad's lips loosened like there was a possibility of a smile inside them.

Juniper jumped on the chance to bring it out. "A dragon, actually. Fifteen feet high! No . . . *twenty*! And it was getting ready to burn the whole kingdom—uh, ranch—down, and everything in it.

You, me, Mom, Rose—everyone. Remember what the dragon did in the last episode of *Castle McAvoy*? Able and I couldn't let that happen here. We had to save you guys." She ventured a grin.

"A dragon, huh? In the paddock?"

"A huge one," Juniper said. "The exact size of that tree, in fact." She pointed at the old elm with the claw-like branches.

Her father looked at the tree, then back at Juniper. "So, what you're saying is, if you didn't have to battle a dragon to save our ranch, you would've had Able brushed by now?" He raised one eyebrow, and a giggle bubbled up inside Juniper.

She nodded. "Exactly."

"Okay." Her father whirled around and faced the tree. He stood tall and raised his arms wide.

"Dragon!" her father shouted. "I, King Paul of Ranch Bar K, demand that you halt your threat until…" He paused, glancing at Juniper. "Tomorrow afternoon, after school! Be gone until then, oh fiery dragon … thing."

He turned to Juniper, slapping his hands together like he'd just finished a job well done.

"There. You can pick up where you left off tomorrow, but *after* you've finished your homework." He smiled. "Deal?"

Juniper bowed low. "Your wish is my command, my king."

"Good, because I need Able happy and healthy tomorrow." He rubbed the horse's nose. "He might have a job."

Juniper's eyes grew wide. "Really? You think he's ready?"

Her father nodded. "He's been doing great with you here at the ranch. And this role sounds perfect for him."

"What it is?" Juniper wiggled her fingers back and forth at her side, excitement building within her.

"It's . . ." Her father held on to his next word, and the suspense bit into Juniper.

"What?" she pressed. Then she saw the twinkle in her father's eye.

"Wait! It isn't . . . Is it . . . Do they want him for . . ." Juniper gulped. "*Castle McAvoy?*"

Her father cracked another smile, and Juniper released all her excitement in a jump and an "AAAAHHHH!"

But her father put up his hands. "Don't get too excited. They like his photo, but he hasn't got the part yet. And while he's been doing well with you here, he doesn't have any experience on a set with different handlers. He needs lots of rest tonight so he'll be less stressed tomorrow."

7

"He'll do great." Juniper began to undo the straps of the saddle on Able's back. "Won't you, Able? You'll be the best horse on the show."

"Well, we'll find out when he auditions on the set in the morning," her father said, grabbing a brush and holding it out for Juniper. "You just make him shine."

"I can go with you." Juniper laid her hand on Able's back, her tummy flopping inside her as she willed her father to say yes. "You'll need someone to take care of Able while you're talking to Fay and all the other studio suits."

"You're eleven," her father said. "Eleven-year-olds are in school on Thursdays."

"But Able will need me, especially since it's his first time."

"He'll do just fine with me. Won't you, boy?" Her father rubbed Able's nose, and the horse nickered.

Juniper bit her lip. She had to say something to get her dad to take her. "But there are kids on *Castle McAvoy*, and *they* go to the studio."

"They're actors, and they go to school on the set."

"I could—" she started, but her father cut her off.

"We've talked about this, Junebug. We're the trainers. The animals are the actors in this family." Her father filled up a bucket with water and placed it next to her feet. "I'll come out and say good night to Able when you're done."

He tweaked her ear, then strode toward their house.

Juniper watched him go. "You horses get to do all the fun stuff. You're going to love it, Able. A set for a show is so exciting. Mom and Dad used to take Rose and me when we were little, but now it's all school, school, school. I wish I could go with you."

She brushed dust and mud off Able's sides.

"You're perfect for *Castle McAvoy*. Maybe you'll get to defend the castle. Won't that be fun?"

Able's ears twitched as Juniper started combing his mane. "I wonder if Sir Gregor will ride you. Or Lady Penelope. They're my favorites. Sir Gregor is the bravest of all the knights—and he's funny, too. But Lady Penelope can outsmart anyone. Plus, she's the best with a sword."

Juniper parried with the comb, and Able snorted.

"I wish we had a TV out here so you could see them," she said, lifting one of his hooves to make sure there were no splits or stones. "The best part about the show is, they're all kids like me, battling dragons and trolls and protecting their castle. So amazing! I'd give anything to be in *Castle McAvoy*. Anything!"

When Juniper finished checking Able's hooves,

she dampened a cloth and gently wiped his face.

"I know you'll get the part, Able," she told him. "You're the best at all the tricks. Just remember to breathe, know that you're safe, and Dad will be there the whole time with you."

Able nuzzled Juniper's neck, which made her smile.

"I wish I could go, too. With us together, I know you'd make it onto *Castle McAvoy*. After all, Dad did say you're doing great *with me*." She looked into his deep brown eyes. "I'll think of you all day. I promise."

After giving Able a quick kiss on his nose, Juniper led him into his stall, closed the door, and told him good night.

In her bedroom later, Juniper logged onto the Hoofprints Horse Riding Forum, as she did every night. She wished she could tell someone—tell everyone—about Able's audition, but her dad always said they had to keep quiet until after a role had aired so they don't jinx it. And she definitely didn't want to jinx this.

Holding back her urge, she checked out the new posts, but her mind wasn't on them. She couldn't think of any supportive comment to put on HrseGrl25's bad fall video, and even CutesyHorse's latest Horse in a Hat picture didn't make her laugh. Juniper was too busy worrying.

Able was a great horse, and Juniper loved him more than anything. But her father was right that Able did his best tricks when she was there. She'd seen Able when her dad was working with him, and he was good but got distracted easily. When she was with Able, he held his head higher and trotted with the enthusiasm of a puppy with a new toy.

Juniper sighed. She *really* wanted Able to be on *Castle McAvoy*, but how could she make sure he did his best if she wasn't there?

She flipped through a few more posts, then went to the thread she saved for last every night: Showmanship with Claudia Rains. Claudia posted a picture and inspirational message every day, and Juniper felt that if it was the last thing she saw before she went to sleep, she'd be able to soak up all of Claudia's wisdom and talent in her dreams. Claudia was perfect in every video she posted. She had won more medals at the Greater American Trick Riding Championship than any other rider, and Juniper wanted to be just like her.

But when she gazed at the picture and message Claudia had posted that day, Juniper gasped. In the photo, Claudia was standing next to her horse, Sahara. All their medals were draped on Sahara's back, and on top of the picture were the words "To be successful, you can't let anything stop you. You have to stack the odds in your favor. Do it!"

Juniper thought of Able and how if she was at his audition, the odds would be stacked much more in his favor. She felt like Claudia was speaking just to her, telling her what she had to do.

A plan started to form in Juniper's mind.

Chapter 2
Stowaway

Sitting at the kitchen table the next morning, Juniper felt like a herd of horses were stampeding in her stomach. Her mother had put a steaming plate of pancakes in front of her, but all she could focus on was the scene outside the kitchen window.

Her father was hooking the horse trailer to his truck. She had to get in place before he left, and there wasn't much time.

"Rose, breakfast!" her mother called, then

turned to Juniper. "Not hungry, Junebug? You barely ate last night, too. After all that kingdom-saving you and Able did, I would've thought you'd gobble up a feast this morning. Are you feeling okay?" She reached out to place the back of her hand on Juniper's forehead.

"I feel fine, Mom," Juniper said, jumping up from her chair. "I'll go get Rose."

Juniper couldn't let her mother think she was sick. Her mother would keep too close an eye on her, and Juniper's plan would be ruined. To prove that she was feeling okay, Juniper cut off a large piece of pancake and plopped it into her mouth, then ran upstairs to get her sister.

Rose's room looked like a wardrobe had exploded. Clothes were on the bed, the desk, the beanbag, the dresser. Just about the only place that didn't have clothes was the floor, as though Rose had tried on every outfit she had, then discarded them all carefully. Juniper never thought much about what she was wearing. She usually wore some combination of jeans and a T-shirt. She wondered if she'd care more when she started high school, like Rose had.

Juniper heard the bathroom door open, then Rose appeared in the doorway.

"What are you doing in my room?" Rose's voice was laced with annoyance.

"Looking for you," Juniper said. "Breakfast is ready, and the bus will be here any minute."

"I know. Don't hurry me."

Juniper knew her sister hated to be hurried, but this day was too important. She wished she could tell Rose her plan. *Castle McAvoy* had been her favorite show, too. They had watched it together every Sunday, but that was another thing that changed when her sister started high school. Juniper had to do this alone now.

Rose took a last look at herself in her full-length mirror, puckered her lips as though she wasn't sure she liked what she saw, and grabbed her backpack.

"Come on, then," she said, waving Juniper out of her room before she shut the door behind them.

Juniper followed her sister down the stairs and into the kitchen, glancing out the window to check on her father's progress. The trailer was in place, and her father was nowhere to be seen. Maybe he was getting Able now. She prayed that he'd take a long time.

"See you, Mom," Juniper said, stuffing another big piece of pancake into her mouth.

"Wait! Rose, you haven't eaten."

"I'll get something at school," Rose said, and Juniper said a silent *thank you* in her head.

"At least take some fruit." Their mother picked up an apple from the bowl on the counter and tossed it across the kitchen to Rose, who was already at the back door. Juniper reached out and grabbed it after her sister missed, then placed the apple in Rose's hand.

"Thanks," Rose said, and waved at their mother as Juniper shut the door.

The bus was just pulling up when the sisters got to the bus stop. It was the only bus that came to the houses this far out of town and it was always packed by the time it got to their ranch. As soon as Juniper saw it, the herd in her tummy turned into a whirlwind. This was it. She had to do everything she'd planned perfectly.

Rose began to climb the stairs, and Juniper tugged on her sister's shirt to stop her. "Hey, Rose, I totally forgot. Mrs. Hernandez is picking me up this morning so Cali and I can practice our spelling test."

Rose frowned. "You're not coming on the bus?" She glanced at the faces watching them through the bus windows.

Regret crimped Juniper's chest. Now that they went to different schools, sitting together on the bus was one of the few things they did together outside of home, but she had to give Able his best chance to be on *Castle McAvoy*.

"Have a great day at school," Juniper said, trying to make her voice as cheerful and unsuspicious as possible.

Rose shook her head and climbed on board.

As soon as the bus drove away, Juniper stepped behind the big oak near the bus stop, so she couldn't be seen from their house. She watched until the bus was out of sight, then she stashed her backpack under a sagebrush and snuck back into the ranch.

She could hear her father getting Able out of the stable. She still had time, but she had to be fast!

Juniper dashed to the horse trailer and up the ramp. Quickly, she squeezed into the cabinet at the back of the trailer that held the training and care equipment, shutting the door tightly behind her. She crossed her fingers that her dad wouldn't need to get anything until they were at the studio.

Voices reverberated around the trailer, followed by a *clomp, clomp, clomp* as Able walked in. The horse gave a slight neigh, and Juniper hoped Able wouldn't let on that the trailer had a stowaway. Before long, she heard the truck door shut and the engine roar to life. Then, with a shudder, the trailer began to move.

The studio was about forty-five minutes away, and Juniper was glad the day wasn't too hot. The compartment was stuffy, but at least she could see out the small window in the side door. To pass the time, she thought of all the horse tricks she'd seen on *Castle McAvoy* that Able might be asked to do. Before she knew it, the truck had stopped and her dad was talking to the guard at the studio gate.

Juniper's heartbeat galloped in her chest as the truck pulled into the studio lot. The trailer turned left, then right, then left again, and Juniper watched out the window for the familiar turrets of Castle McAvoy.

Finally, the trailer stopped, and Juniper rubbed her clammy hands on her jeans. Her father was not going to be happy to see her, and the crimp in her chest pinched harder. This was the only way to show him that she could help. She had to take the chance.

Her father's truck door opened and closed. "I'll be right back, Able."

Juniper carefully climbed out of the cabinet, and

Able nuzzled her neck.

"You knew I was in there the whole time, didn't you?" she asked the horse, rubbing his nose. "Pray that Dad isn't too mad. But even if he is, when he sees you get that part because I'm here, he'll forgive me. I hope."

Juniper peered out of the trailer at the studio parking lot. A trolley carrying tourists rattled by, and some waved at her like she belonged there. A wave of excitement sprang up Juniper's spine.

"I'll bring him around." Her father's voice was followed by his footsteps getting closer. The stampede of nervous horses in Juniper's tummy pounded faster.

She heard a click, then the back doors of the trailer swung open. "All right, Able, you're— Juniper!"

Her father's eyes grew wide when he spotted her.

She gave him her best smile. "Hi, Dad. Don't worry about Able. He's going to do great in his audition. I was just telling him how wonderful he is, and . . ."

Juniper trailed off. Was that smoke coming out of her father's ears? If it wasn't, it could've been. He twisted his arms across his chest tight enough to squeeze a flea. She waited for his outburst, ready to explain, to plead for mercy, to beg him to understand.

But instead of exploding, he narrowed his eyes.

That was so much worse.

"You're supposed to be in school." His voice was low and gravelly. "What did I tell you last night—"

"I know, but Able really needed me. You said he did better with me around, and—"

"Are you ready, Paul?" A tall, slender woman walked up to the trailer with a clipboard in her hand. When she got close, she peered inside, and

24

a smile lit up her face. "Juniper? Is that you? Little Junie?"

Juniper grinned. Her father couldn't be angry with her now, at least not in front of the casting lady.

"Hi, Fay." Juniper gave her a wave.

"I haven't seen you in years," Fay said. "You're growing so big."

Juniper wanted to roll her eyes. Was that all grown-ups ever noticed? She had to keep Fay on track. "You're going to love Able. He can do any trick you want. He's amazing. Right, Able?" She patted Able's nose, and he seemed to nicker in agreement.

"That's exactly what we need." Fay smiled brightly. "Let's head over to the set and see him in action."

Under a deep frown, Juniper's father whispered, "We're going to talk about this later." Then he turned to Fay with a grin. "We're on our way."

Juniper grabbed the lead rope and clipped it to Able's halter. Then they were out of the trailer and following Fay around the back of the big studio buildings.

With her father and Fay walking ahead, Juniper guided Able and tried to keep her heart from racing straight out of her chest. She had to stay calm and professional, just like she'd seen her father do when she'd joined him on sets when she was little. But as soon as they turned the corner of the studio, Juniper lost all her composure. She froze, sucking in a breath, then managed to squeak out, "That's it, Able. That's it!"

The main courtyard of Castle McAvoy stood before them. The tall stone walls of the castle surrounded a huge opening laid out with packed dirt, hay bales, and tufts of grass. It was just like Juniper had seen on TV, except one big difference:

When she gazed up, there were no towers or turrets—just a huge, bright green screen.

"This is Castle McAvoy, Able," she whispered into his ear. "You're going to be on the show. I can feel it."

Able nodded like he knew it, too.

"We just need to see Able on the set," Fay said, halting a few feet from the packed dirt. "We'll have him walk, gallop, do a few jumps. That sort of thing. Sound good?"

"No problem," Juniper's father said. He grabbed Able's lead rope and turned to Juniper, eyes as serious as an arrow aimed at its target. "Stand over there, out of the way, and don't say a word."

"But, Dad—"

"Ah!" Her father lifted one finger. "Don't make me send you to wait in the truck, because I will."

Juniper clamped her mouth shut. She ran her

hand encouragingly down Able's neck, then walked to the spot where her father had pointed. Stuffing her hands deep into her pockets, she watched as her dad walked Able around the large set.

"He's a beautiful horse," Fay said. "Ben, what do you think?" She nodded to a man who was striding up from the main building. A boy walked at his side, and Juniper wondered if he was one of the actors. He was taller than Juniper; older, but not much. She couldn't recognize him, though, and she felt sure she knew every face that had ever been on the show.

Ben and the boy stopped next to Fay. Ben whistled. "Great-looking. He's just what we need. If he can jump well, of course."

If he can jump, Juniper thought. Able could jump better than any horse on the show.

Her heart raced a little faster. She was even more sure Able was going to get this part.

Fay turned to Juniper's dad. "Paul, Marcus is one of our stunt riders." She pointed to the boy, who stepped forward. "Let's have him take Able around the courtyard."

"Sure," Juniper's father said. "Hey, Marcus. Able will be nice to you." He smiled big, and Marcus mirrored his expression.

Juniper watched nervously as the boy mounted Able and took him for a light trot on the dirt. Able looked good, his head high, and Juniper's chest filled with pride. Marcus pushed Able faster, and he obeyed. Then Marcus took the horse for a small jump over a hay bale, but Able resisted.

Juniper straightened. It wasn't a difficult jump. Why had Able hesitated? Marcus tried again, and this time Able did the jump, but it hadn't looked pretty.

She glanced at her father. His cheek stuck out

like it did when he gritted his teeth hard. He was worried.

"Go again," Fay called to Marcus, and the boy took Able around the courtyard again. He lined them up with the hay bale and began the jump, but Able again resisted, making a jump that looked clumsy.

Ben shook his head slightly. "I don't know. He's a good-looking horse, but I don't think he's—"

"I'll show you!" The words were out of Juniper's mouth before she could regret saying them. When her father turned to her as though he might breathe fire, she knew she'd probably made a big mistake. But it was too late now. And if there was anything she could do to help Able get this part, she had to do it.

"Able's really not a bad jumper," Juniper continued, hurrying over to her horse. "He's usually great. But this is his first time on a set, so he's nervous. I can show you what he can do. I know you're going to love him."

Juniper knew she was babbling, but she was as nervous as Able was.

"Well," Fay started, "you can try, but—"

"Great!" Juniper didn't wait for any more words. As soon as Marcus had dismounted, Juniper swung herself onto Able's back. She leaned down, patted his neck, and said, "You can do this, Able. I believe in you."

Able nodded his head, making Juniper smile.

She could feel the energy running through Able. With her on his back, he was comfortable and excited to show off.

Juniper gave his reins a quick tug, and they cantered around the courtyard. She walked Able backward, then pulled him up to rear. Eyeing the hay bale, Juniper lined up Able, and they soared over. Then she trotted him to where Fay, Marcus, Ben, and Juniper's father were standing. Able finished with a one-legged bow.

Everyone was smiling broadly now, then Juniper heard applause. She looked up and saw a group of people at the door of the main studio. There were grown-ups and some children. Juniper immediately recognized the kid actors Caleb Donovan, who played Sir Gregor, and Alicia Hernandez, who played Lady Penelope. They were watching her!

"You were right, Juniper," Fay said. "Able does move beautifully. I guess he just needed the right rider."

"Hey," Marcus protested, and Juniper had a stab of worry that he felt insulted. But when she glanced at him, Marcus was smiling. He didn't seem to mind that she'd brought more out of Able than he had.

"I'd be happy to help," Juniper said, then cringed inwardly. Her father would not like that she offered. But if it made the difference between Able getting the job and not getting the job, it had to be worth it, hadn't it?

Fay turned to Juniper's father. "Thanks for bringing Able, Paul. He's everything you said he was, and more. We've got another horse to look at, but I'll let you know."

"Great," Juniper's father said, nodding to Juniper to get down. "Let me know if you need anything else. Come on, Juniper, let's get Able home."

On the drive back to their ranch, Juniper sat in the passenger seat of her dad's truck instead of cramped inside the trailer's equipment cabinet. Her father didn't say a word the entire trip, and Juniper knew that was a bad sign. The quieter her dad got, the angrier he was. But nothing could wipe the giant smile off her face.

She had ridden her horse on a TV set and done well. She wanted to do that every day for the rest of her life.

Later that night, as Juniper sat with her family around their dinner table, Rose pestered her with questions about the set, and Juniper was all too happy to tell her everything. Their father did not think it was fun.

"I told you to stay quiet and out of the way," he said, lowering the piece of garlic bread he'd been bringing to his lips. "You don't listen, Juniper. This isn't a game. It's not showing off for your friends. This is my work."

"I just wanted to help," Juniper said.

"But you didn't. You showed them that Able can only work well with you, but on a set, he's got to be able to work well with other stunt riders and the actors." Anger filled every word. "I trusted that Able would get there with Marcus, but now, they'll never know. You might've cost us the job."

Juniper opened her mouth to answer, but when her dad's cell phone rang, she shut her mouth again.

Her father walked into his office to take the call, and Juniper sank into her seat. She'd only been trying to help. She hadn't thought that she could've ruined Able's audition, and now . . . maybe she had.

"He's just in a bad mood," Rose said, twirling spaghetti onto her fork. "I think you did the right thing, Junie."

"Your father's not in a bad mood," their mother said. "He's taking care of you. He doesn't want you to get hurt."

"Juniper's one of the best riders around," Rose said, and Juniper looked at her in surprise. They used to ride together all the time, but ever since

Rose started high school, she acted like riding was for babies. Juniper didn't think Rose had seen her ride in months, but here she was, cheering her on.

"He's got his reasons for keeping you away from the set," their mother said. "You need to trust him."

"But Mom . . . ," Rose began but stopped when the door to their father's office opened and he walked out.

His phone was in his hand, and he had a grim look on his face.

"That was Fay," he said, and Juniper's heart sank. She had ruined Able's audition. She had ruined everything.

"They want Able for the role," he said.

"That's wonderful," her mother said.

"And they want Juniper to stunt as well," her father said.

Juniper looked at her dad in astonishment. Had

he just said what she thought he'd said? Had he just said . . .

Rose squealed, squeezing Juniper in a hug. That was when Juniper realized she had heard right.

"I'm going to be on *Castle McAvoy*?"

Juniper squealed, too.

Chapter 3
First Day on Set

The morning of her first day on the set of *Castle McAvoy*, Juniper could barely control her excitement. She was filled to the brim, and her fingers continuously twitched, even after she put her hands into her pockets.

Her parents had been reluctant to allow her to go. Her father kept giving her his "the animals are the actors in this family" line, and her mother was worried about school and safety and security—all things Juniper was sure would be okay. Finally, it wasn't Juniper's begging and promising that she'd stay on top of schoolwork that changed her parents' minds. It was Rose reminding them that this was Able's big break, and he'd gotten it because of Juniper.

Now Juniper felt as though she had to prove to her parents that they had nothing to worry about, that she wouldn't let them down. She had to help Able be his best, and she had to be perfect at all her own stunts, just like Claudia Rains was perfect with her tricks.

But as Juniper and Able walked with her father from their truck to the set, the stampede of nervous horses returned to Juniper's tummy.

"I'll be with you the whole time," her father told her, "but make sure you don't do anything dangerous. I don't want you doing any trick you haven't done lots of times before. Okay?"

"Yes, Dad."

"Take your time. If they need to do a few takes, that's okay."

"Yes, Dad."

"Just breathe and concentrate and—"

"Dad!" Juniper squeezed Able's lead rope. "You're making us more nervous. Right, Able?"

Able shook like he was trying to get the worrying thoughts out of his head.

"All right." Juniper's father nodded. "Just be careful."

"We will."

Juniper plastered an uneasy smile on her face, but it quickly drained away. The studio was filled with much more activity than when they'd come for the audition. People rushed about—some in costumes, some carrying lights, some pushing carts full of props. Able's ears pricked up and rocked from side to side, listening to all the strange noises. Juniper rubbed his neck to ease him, hoping the soft movement would calm the herd in her stomach, too.

"Juniper!"

Marcus hurried over, and Juniper felt relieved to see a familiar face.

"Hey, Marcus."

"Welcome to Castle McAvoy." He grinned. "Let me show you where we'll be rehearsing today. We've got a lot to go through."

"I'm going to get all the paperwork signed, Junie," her dad said. "Don't do anything until I get back, okay?"

"Dad, I'll be fine." Inwardly, she rolled her eyes, but she was pretty sure her father got the message from the tone of her words. She didn't want Marcus to think she was a baby who needed to be protected.

She was a TV stuntperson now.

If her father was offended, he didn't show it. Concern was written all over his face. "I won't be long," he said, then headed off toward the studio.

"Parents!" Juniper said to Marcus once her dad was out of earshot.

He chuckled. "It's nice that he's worried. I don't think my parents ever worry about what I'm doing."

"They don't?"

Marcus shook his head. "They run the stunt team for the show. Remember Ben from your audition?"

Juniper nodded.

"He's my dad. He just wants me to hit my mark, every time." Marcus laughed again.

"Wow! You're so lucky. It's my dream to be here. And I owe it all to Able." Juniper rubbed her horse's nose.

"Nah. You were great. You both were." Marcus

leaned toward Able to make sure he got the compliment, too.

Marcus led them to an open field beyond the courtyard. Barriers had been set up in the same large semicircle as the courtyard, and blocks were in place where the hay bales had been.

"We work out the stunt scenes here while they're filming other scenes on the real set," Marcus said. He took them to the far side, where a black horse a few hands taller than Able was hitched to a pole.

"This is Zombie. She's been with my family since she was born." Marcus reached into his pocket and pulled out a baggie with apple slices. He gave one to Zombie and one to Juniper.

"Hi, Zombie." Juniper lifted her palm, with the apple slice on it, up to the older horse. "She's beautiful. Why'd you call her Zombie?"

Marcus laughed. "When she was a foal, she fell

in love with a big rubber eyeball we had put out for Halloween. She played with it and slept with it, so we figured that if she loved eyeballs that much, she must be a zombie."

Juniper giggled. "At least she doesn't act like a zombie," she said as the horse nibbled the apple slice off Juniper's palm.

Marcus shook his head. "Nah. She's really easygoing. We'll work together, so Able can get used to being with her. Zombie's in most of the horse scenes on this show, so she can keep Able comfortable."

"Okay," Juniper said. This was it. She and Able were going to do their first stunts on *Castle McAvoy*.

"You're going to be great," Juniper whispered into Able's ear. She hoped she'd be great, too. Able snorted. He was ready for some action.

Juniper and Able followed Marcus and Zombie

around the made-up courtyard, through archways and over boxes. They started slow but quickly picked up the pace. Zombie was a good teacher to Able, encouraging him with nickers, and Able was happy to follow.

Juniper couldn't have been happier if someone was feeding her a lifetime supply of chocolate cake. When Marcus brought them to a stop, she couldn't get rid of the broad smile on her face.

"That was great," said a girl sitting cross-legged on the ground just outside the rehearsal area. A boy was standing next to her, and they were both watching Juniper and Able. Juniper sucked in a nervous breath. How long had they been there?

"Hey, Leigh." Marcus jumped off Zombie. "Hey, Pablo. This is Juniper and Able." He glanced at Juniper and added, "Leigh and Pablo are on the stunt team, too."

"Hi," Juniper squeaked, hating how small her voice sounded.

No one seemed to notice, though. Leigh jumped up to pet Able's nose, and Pablo said, "You guys are naturals. That was a good run."

The stampede inside Juniper's tummy turned into a fluttering, and she hoped she wasn't blushing.

"He's beautiful," Leigh said, smiling at Able. "Have you tried the costumes on him yet?"

"My plan next." Marcus grinned.

"Good. We got here in time." Leigh smiled even wider at Juniper. "This is my favorite part. The horses look so good in their costumes."

Juniper liked Leigh immediately.

Marcus rummaged through a box on the side of the rehearsal area, pulling out rump covers, chest pieces, saddles, and more.

"I recognize these." Juniper picked up a bright

blue blanket with yellow edging. "They're Lady Penelope's from a couple seasons ago."

"Wow. You must be a big fan to remember that," Pablo said.

"Who isn't?" Juniper asked. "You know you guys work on the absolute best show, right?"

Leigh nodded her head. "And now you do, too. It's so fun!" She lifted up an ornate metal headpiece with turquoise stones. "Let's put these on Able."

Juniper, Marcus, Leigh, and Pablo dressed up Able and Zombie, and the horses didn't mind the attention one bit. They nickered, and Able lifted his hooves, ready to run again.

"Are you guys horsing around?"

Juniper turned and gasped. A group of kids had walked up, and at the front were Caleb Donovan and Alicia Hernandez. Caleb was laughing.

"Very funny, Caleb," Marcus said, but he didn't

sound like he found it funny at all. "This is Juniper Brown, new to the horse stunt team. And this is her horse, Able."

He introduced all the actors, and Juniper nodded to each one, her voice stuck in her throat. She had been watching Sir Gregor, Lady Penelope, and the other characters on *Castle McAvoy* for so long, she felt as though they were old friends. She had to remind herself that she was meeting these kids for the very first time.

Finally, Juniper squeaked out, "Hi. I'm such a big fan. I can't believe I'm meeting you. I love everything about this show. When you killed that giant beetle troll at the end of last season, I cheered so hard. The bug guts you got on you were so gross." Juniper realized she was rambling and clamped her mouth shut. It was hard not to gush, though. She felt like excitement was bursting under her skin.

Alicia scrunched up her nose. "Ugh. I was finding that stuff in my hair for days after we shot that scene. It really was gross."

"It probably didn't help that I kept putting it in your hair when you weren't looking." Caleb stayed serious for about a second, then bent over laughing.

"That was you?" Alicia play-slapped Caleb's arm, but laughed, too. "Watch out for Caleb, Juniper. He hasn't yet found a prank he doesn't love."

Juniper grinned. She wasn't sure she liked the idea of being at the other end of one of Caleb's pranks, but she definitely liked being friends with her favorite actors.

"So, can you do all the twirling and jumping and things these guys can do?" Alicia asked, pointing at Leigh, Marcus, and Pablo.

Juniper nodded, pushing down the twinge she felt in her tummy. She had done well in their audition and knew she could do lots of good tricks at home, but now, being on the set, she was starting to get nervous she wouldn't be good enough.

"Wow," Alicia said. "Don't get me wrong, I think horses are really cool, but I hate when I have to get on them. It's so high and scary. You can do all the action parts any day."

A loudspeaker crackled outside the studio building, and Alicia grabbed Caleb's sleeve. "Come on, I'm not going to be late to costume again because of you."

"Ooh, I wonder if Anne has found the cockroach I left in her thread drawer yet." Caleb cackled again, and Alicia shook her head.

"See you around, Juniper," Alicia said, then dragged Caleb away.

"I had no idea Lady Penelope was scared of horses," Juniper said, watching the actors head back to the studio. "She does all the best stunts."

Leigh laughed. "That's because when Lady Penelope's on a horse, she's played by me."

"Yeah, Leigh makes Alicia look really good on a horse," Marcus said. "Right, Zombie?" He rubbed his horse's shoulder.

Juniper gave a small smile but couldn't stop wondering if she was going to make an actor look really good on a horse like Leigh did one day.

"All right, let's give Able a run with all this gear on, make sure he's comfortable," Marcus said.

Able looked amazing with the costume on. And riding him, Juniper felt like a princess, but a warrior princess who was protecting her castle, just like in the show. Pablo, Leigh, and Marcus watched from the side, cheering them on.

When Juniper's father walked up, he was smiling from ear to ear.

Juniper pulled up alongside him. "Able loves the costume. Pablo says he's a natural."

"Of course he is!" her father said, waving at Pablo and Leigh. He turned back to Juniper. "And you look good up there, too. You having fun?"

"The most fun," Juniper said.

"Good." Her father looked over Able protectively, checking for any cuts or other small injuries. "He looks great. I'm proud of you, Junie."

Juniper's heart swelled. "Thanks, Dad."

"Just be careful and don't—"

"Do anything dangerous," Juniper finished. "I know."

"Let's get lunch," Marcus said, bringing Zombie over. "You've got costume fittings at one."

"Costume fittings," Juniper's dad said. Then he tweaked her ear when she was back on the ground. "It sounds like you are a star already. Lunch sounds great. It will be my treat."

"Isn't food free on the set?" Juniper asked.

Her father winked. "That's why I'm treating."

Juniper and Marcus laughed as they walked the horses to the stable.

Juniper's afternoon was busy. In the costume department, every part of her body was measured and recorded so costumes for multiple characters could be tailored to fit her. Able was fitted for his costumes, too. Then Marcus and Zombie showed them all the different sets the show used, the tricks they filmed most often, and tips on doing stunts for the camera.

Doing tricks with Able for *Castle McAvoy* was very different from training in their pasture at home. On the set, not only did she have to do the trick right, she had to make sure Able was where the director wanted him for the camera shot. If he wasn't in the right place, or she wasn't in the best position, they'd have to do it again. And if they had to do it too many times, they'd mess up the schedule. Marcus had told her this over and over: "Don't slow down the production schedule!" Juniper had spray-painted it on a billboard in her mind so she'd never forget.

That evening, as her father drove her and Able home, Juniper was so tired, she fell asleep in the truck. Her energy picked up when they got home. Her mother and Rose came running out of their house and smothered her in a big hug.

Rose was full of questions. "What were the actors like? What stunts did you do? Did you get to wear those awesome dresses?"

"Let her take a breath," their mother said as Juniper hurried to answer. But Juniper didn't mind all the questions. They made her bloom inside. She'd missed Rose's attention, and she was getting it now all thanks to *Castle McAvoy*.

Juniper had to make sure it stayed that way.

While the sisters readied Able for bed, Juniper answered all of Rose's questions.

"Able was the real star. You should've seen him on the set. He knew he belonged there. He looks really good in his costume, too." She kissed Able on the nose and whispered, "Good night, sweet prince. You're going to be great again tomorrow."

"Do you think I could bring my friends to the set?" Rose asked as they walked back to the house.

"We can't tell anyone until Able and I are on the show, remember?" Juniper said. "Dad says it'll jinx it. Like that time he announced that Lucky would be in *A Sunday Horse*, and they cut all her scenes. We can't tell anyone about Able and me, even though I want to."

Rose nodded, but she didn't look happy about it.

By the time they got to the dinner table, Juniper had just enough energy left to wolf down the black bean chili her mom had made. Then she climbed into her own bed, waved at Able's stable through her window, and was asleep before her head dropped onto her pillow.

Chapter 4
Camera Time

Juniper's days did not get easier. Between all the different stunts, the sets, and the costumes, there was so much to learn and get right. And that was just for the show.

She also had classes every day with Mr. Vela and the other kids from the studio. Juniper held in a secret laugh when Mr. Vela opened his desk drawer and a bunch of plastic flowers popped out. Caleb must've rigged it.

Finally, after weeks of rehearsal, Marcus told Juniper she'd be riding for the camera. She and Able would be in a scene that would be in an episode—of her favorite show ever!

The night before her on-camera debut, the stampede raced in Juniper's stomach all through dinner. To celebrate, her mother had made her favorite veggie tacos, with baked apple doughnuts for dessert, but Juniper couldn't even enjoy them. She was too excited—and nervous.

"You're going to be okay, you know," her mother told her as they put away the leftovers.

Juniper glanced at her out of the corner of her eye. "What are you talking about?"

"You think I don't notice when my daughter's nervous? You ate one bite of one doughnut, when I usually have to keep the plate away from you because you'll devour the whole stack. Plus, you just put the salsa in the dishwasher."

Juniper opened the dishwasher door, and sure enough, there was the jar was sitting there. She sighed, pulling the jar out and placing the salsa where it belonged in the fridge.

"Sorry." Juniper hadn't wanted to let on that she was nervous. She wanted her parents to think she could do the stunts without any problems. "I just want to do a good job."

"And you will," her mother said. "Remember that night when they called your father to hire you?"

Juniper nodded.

"Rose said you are a great rider, and she's right. You've got it in your blood, just like your father."

"He is a really good trainer," Juniper said.

"Not only that—he used to be one of the best trick riders around. But that's a story for another time." Her mother took the dish towel out of

Juniper's hands. "You need to get some rest for your big day. I'll finish up here."

"Okay, Mom. Thank you."

"And Junebug . . ."

"Yeah?"

"I'm so proud of you." Her mother enveloped Juniper in a big hug. "You will be the star of the show."

Juniper smiled.

Tucked into bed that night, Juniper tried to sleep. She was tired, but her mind kept racing with all the rules and tips Marcus had given her. Finally, when sleep wouldn't come, she logged onto the Hoofprints Horse Riding Forum. It was the first time that she'd logged on since she'd started working with *Castle McAvoy*. She'd been too tired every night before, but now she needed some inspiration.

Juniper giggled at CutesyHorse's picture of her

horse, Shadow, in a Cat in the Hat hat. She posted a "yay" sticker under the video of HrseGrl25 finally jumping without falling. And she put a smiley under JessicaRides4Ever's painting of her horse Willy. Finally, she went to Claudia Rains's thread. Claudia's latest post was a picture of a horseshoe and the words "Don't forget: The world is lucky to have you."

Juniper smiled to herself. "The world is lucky to have me," she whispered, quieting the stampede in her stomach. Lying back down on her pillow, she glanced out the window at the stable across the pasture. "The show is lucky to have us, Able. We'll be fine. Better than fine. We'll be great."

At last, Juniper drifted off to sleep.

When her father rapped on her bedroom door the next morning, Juniper was already up, dressed, and ready to tackle the day. The herd in her stomach was still busy, but now the horses were prancing with excitement as well as nerves. She was going to be on *Castle McAvoy*!

Able was ready, too. He snorted when he strode into the trailer and nickered when he walked out to the studio lot. This was their big day, and he knew it.

As they walked to the stables, Juniper's mind whirled with all the tips she had been telling herself to not forget. Her phone pinged in her backpack.

"That might be Mom," she told her dad. "Go ahead with Able. I'll catch up."

She pulled out her phone, but the message wasn't from her mother. It was from her friend Cali.

Cali: *OMG! You're on Castle McAvoy! I can't believe you didn't tell me. I want to hear everything.*

Juniper's eyes widened. How had Cali found out? She had told her she was tutoring at home for a bit to help her dad. She texted back.

Sorry! I'm not supposed to say anything. It's so awesome. I'll fill you in as soon as I can.

Stuffing her phone into her backpack, Juniper ran to catch up with her dad and Able, hoping her father wasn't right that telling people would jinx it.

Soon, Juniper and Able were both costumed and standing at the side of the set for their on-camera debut.

Her dad gave her a big kiss on her forehead. "Go get them, Junebug. Just breathe, and remember everything we've been working on."

Juniper nodded.

"And be careful," her dad said.

"We will," Juniper said, tamping down her nerves.

"Places for the catch scene!" Tomas, the production assistant, shouted.

Ben sauntered over to Juniper and Able. "Are

you guys ready to go out there?"

Juniper tried to ignore the stampede in her belly.

"Do everything like you've been doing it in rehearsals, and we'll have this wrapped up quickly." Ben smiled big, then helped Juniper lead Able to his starting position on the other side of the courtyard entrance.

They had rehearsed under all the lights and in costume, but Juniper didn't remember it being as hot as she felt now. Sitting on Able's back, she took in a deep breath and glanced at her dad on the sidelines. He gave her a smile and a thumbs-up.

The trick wasn't difficult. It was something she and Able had done lots of times in their pasture at home. They'd also done it fine in rehearsal.

But now, Juniper could see that every eye was on her and her horse. Marcus and Pablo were hidden in the set, ready for their parts, and Leigh was on the edge of the set, waiting to shoot a scene of her own immediately afterward. Even Alicia, Caleb, and the other actors were watching. Alicia gave Juniper a wave, and she smiled nervously back.

Suddenly, there was no more time to think about how she'd do. The director, Sadie Aprell, shouted, "Action!" and Juniper spurred Able forward.

Through the courtyard entrance they galloped, then around the pathway marked out on the ground. Other actors leaped from behind walls and hay bales, reaching out as though they wanted to pull Juniper off. Like she'd practiced, she leaned this way, then that, acting like she was trying to get away.

When they got close to the courtyard exit, Marcus stuck out his arm and caught Juniper's boot. Her leg flailed on the side of Able, stopping the horse. Juniper pulled and got her boot away. Then she swung her leg over Able's back so she was sitting with a foot in one stirrup as Able rode her away to safety.

"Cut!" Sadie shouted, and as if the whole set had been holding in their breath, everyone started chattering again.

Marcus and Juniper's dad applauded, and soon, everyone else had joined in. Leigh let out a "Whoop!"

Juniper brought Able back around to the front of the set, grinning from ear to ear. They had survived their first on-camera stunt. Now they just had to hear from the director if it was good.

Rubbing Able's shoulder, Juniper turned toward Sadie, who was watching the footage on a screen next to the camera.

Sadie's eyes were narrowed, and Juniper waited anxiously. Finally, after what seemed like an eternity, a big smile broke out on Sadie's face. "Great job, Juniper and Able. Tomas, that rock isn't in the best position for the shot. Let's move it forward. Juniper, can you guys do that again?"

Juniper felt like her heart might explode with happiness. They were doing the stunt again, but not because of her—not because she and Able had messed up. Sadie had even said they did a great job. She nodded quickly. "Sure!"

"Good. Give us a couple minutes to reset."

"We did it, Able," Juniper told him. "We were good. I hope you feel as amazing as I do."

Once everything was ready, they did the stunt again, then a third time because one of the other actors tripped. Each time, Able and Juniper did their part with no problems, and they didn't mess up the schedule.

Marcus, Pablo, and Leigh surrounded Juniper and Able when they were done, cheering and throwing "Congratulations" and "You did it" into the air. Juniper's dad joined the celebration. He had tears in his eyes, but he quickly blinked them away. It didn't bother Juniper, though. Right then, nothing could.

Chapter 5
Being the Best

Once Sadie said they were done, Juniper took Able for a well-earned rest and some water.

"That was amazing," Juniper told Able as she took off his costume. She brushed him down, then gave him a big hug. "I feel like I could fly, I'm so excited. You were incredible."

Able nodded, making Juniper laugh.

"Places! Silence, please!" Juniper heard over the loudspeakers.

"They're doing the next scene. I'm going to watch Leigh. I'll be right back." Juniper gave Able a kiss on his nose, then ran back to the courtyard and stood next to Ben and her dad to watch.

Leigh was dressed in Sir Gregor's clothes and had a wig to match Caleb's hair. She stood on a ledge hanging over the courtyard.

"You ready, Leigh?" Sadie called up.

"Ready!" Leigh shouted cheerfully.

"All right. Action!"

There was a pause, then a huge shout went up from behind the courtyard walls. Then more shouts and the stamping of feet. Suddenly, a horde of actors burst through the back entrance, running through the courtyard. In the middle of them was Zombie. Juniper could see Marcus crouched, running along with Zombie and guiding her, although he looked like one of the crowd.

One of the actors shouted, "Up there!" and pointed to Leigh. She backed up, hit the castle wall, then glanced around. She had nowhere to go. She was trapped.

The rest of the crowd below began shouting at her. They pointed and snarled and moved in her direction. They wanted to get her down, get Sir Gregor down. They wanted to hurt him.

When Zombie was in position, Leigh jumped off the ledge—over the heads of the actors—and landed gently on Zombie's bare back. But she didn't let her legs dangle on either side, where the mob could grab them. Instead, she stayed crouched on Zombie, grabbing her mane. As Zombie ran around the courtyard, Leigh stood, balancing and staying away from the hands trying to grab her. Then, when Zombie and Leigh had a small lead, she sank onto Zombie's back and sped through the exit, waving her arm in the air.

"Cut!" Sadie shouted. "That was fantastic, Leigh, as always. Let me have a quick look, but I think we've got it."

Juniper let out a breath she hadn't realized she'd been holding. She was about to say "wow," but her father beat her to it.

"Wow. She's a pro, Ben."

Ben nodded. "Yeah, Leigh's the best. She's got a gymnastics background."

"Her balance and agility . . ." Juniper's father whistled. "She's a great find."

Juniper looked from her father to Ben, who were both still watching Leigh as she climbed down from Zombie's back. Juniper smiled, but the smile didn't stay long. She was happy her new friend had done her stunt so well, but Juniper couldn't help wonder: Had her father and Ben said that about her?

She wanted them to.

She'd have to make sure they did.

But how?

When Juniper, Able, and her dad arrived back at their ranch that evening, they saw balloons spelling the word CONGRATULATIONS in big, bright, shimmering colors tied to the gate.

"That's for you guys," her father said, beaming over at her. "We're very proud of you."

Happiness blossomed within Juniper, and she smiled back, pushing down the pinch of fear and uncertainty she'd been feeling ever since she'd watched Leigh's amazing stunt.

"Do you see the balloons, Able?" Juniper asked when they walked out of the trailer. "Aren't they beautiful?"

Able neighed. He liked them, too.

Rose and their mom rushed out of the house and

over to the stable, enveloping Juniper in a huge hug.

"Your father said you were brilliant." Her mother's smile took over her whole face. Juniper felt like the sun was beaming back at her.

"You're going to be on TV for real now," Rose said. "All our friends will see you on *Castle McAvoy*."

Juniper laughed. "Yes. I'll be disguised, but—"

"We'll tell everyone which one is you." Rose hugged Juniper again. "Besides, they'll see Able." She rubbed along his neck.

"It seems like some people know already," Juniper whispered to her sister as she started to brush Able. "Cali texted me."

Rose gulped. "Oh, that was probably my fault. I was excited and told Kim, and she probably told Cali's sister."

"But the jinx," Juniper said.

Rose shrugged. "Obviously there is none,

because you did great." She beamed at her sister.

"Give Able some extra apples before you say goodnight," Juniper's father said as he headed out of the stable. "He earned them. And hurry, your mom's got dinner ready."

When he was gone, Rose slipped her phone out of her pocket. "Come on, let me take a picture of my favorite TV stars. Kim wanted to see you two together."

Juniper was still worried about the jinx, but she loved spending all this time with her sister. She couldn't give that up. She posed next to Able, nuzzling his head with hers, as Rose snapped a bunch of pictures.

"Perfect!" Rose said. "Look."

She swiped through all the photos of Able and Juniper, and Juniper had to admit they were great. Maybe there really wasn't a jinx. How could there be, when this meant she had got her sister back?

Over dinner, Rose asked a million questions about the shoot. Juniper answered them all cheerfully, but her heart wasn't completely in it. The conversation her dad and Ben had had about Leigh played over and over in her head.

"She's a pro," her dad had said.

"Leigh's the best," Ben had said.

Deep down, Juniper knew it wasn't a competition. She and Leigh were part of a team, all of them making the show great with their stunts. And everyone had praised her stunt, too.

So why couldn't she shake the feeling that she had to do better?

As soon as dinner was over, Juniper said she was tired, then went to her bedroom. It had been a long day, and she felt drained, but more than that, she felt uneasy. What if she wasn't as good as Leigh at the stunts? Would they stop putting her on the show? She couldn't risk that. Not only was it her dream come true, it seemed to be her sister's as well. She didn't want to disappoint Rose.

Juniper logged on to the Hoofprints Horse Riding Forum and found Claudia Rains's thread, hoping it would make her feel better. That day, Claudia had posted a video of herself and her horse, Sahara, doing a new trick. While Sahara was galloping around a ring, Claudia climbed beneath Sahara's belly. Then, with one leg hooked under the saddle straps, Claudia leaned out from the side, spreading her arms out wide. She was wearing a shirt with broad sleeves that made it look like she had wings.

It was perfect.

In her caption for the video, Claudia had typed: "Always be your best."

Juniper shut off her computer and tucked herself

into bed. She didn't know if she could be as good as Leigh or Claudia Rains.

What if her best wasn't good enough?

In all her rehearsals the following week, Juniper tried her best, but something was off. She missed a cue for her and Able to walk into a scene. She dropped a prop while they trotted across the courtyard. And she even slipped while doing a stunt that should've been easy. Afterward, when she saw Ben and Sadie talking in hushed tones, Juniper worried that they were talking about her, saying she wasn't good enough to be on the show anymore.

Marcus walked up to her while Juniper was freshening Able's water. "Hey, I just wanted to check on you. You didn't hurt yourself when you slipped, did you?"

"No," Juniper said quickly, even though she had banged her knee on a wall. "I'm fine."

Marcus smiled. "Good. We wouldn't want one of our star stunt kids getting injured."

"Star?" Juniper didn't feel much like a star.

"Of course you are. We have only the best on this show."

Juniper smiled, but the herd in her stomach started to stamp their hooves.

"I've got to go to my next rehearsal, but I'll see you at class later, right?" Marcus asked.

Juniper nodded. When Marcus was out of earshot, she turned back to Able, leaning against his side.

"I'm scared, Able," she said. "Marcus said they have only the best on this show. I've done only one on-camera stunt so far. If I can't be the best, will they make me leave *Castle McAvoy*?"

Able shook his head and sidestepped closer to Juniper, nudging her as if to say no. But Juniper didn't feel so sure.

Tears pricked her eyes, and she brushed them away quickly.

"If they want the best," she said, "that's just what I'll have to be."

She hugged her horse. "Thanks for listening, Able. You're the best friend a girl could want."

After her tutoring class later that day, Juniper cut through the studio building to meet her dad. She smiled as she walked past the set of Lady Penelope and Sir Gregor's war room, then the set of the kitchen where they seemed to make the tastiest food. The sets were empty now, and seeing the lights hanging above them took away some of the magic Juniper felt when she saw the show on TV, but it was still special.

Suddenly, she heard talking. She hurried on, then saw Ben and Sadie in the production office.

They were staring at storyboards pinned to the wall, and the door was open wide.

"I'd love to have something bigger," Sadie said, her back to the door from where Juniper peered inside.

"Like what?" Ben crossed his arms over his chest.

"I don't know, but it's going to the big final scene of this whole storyline, when Lady Penelope rescues Sir Gregor. The stunt has to be more spectacular than anything viewers have seen this season. Or in any other season."

Ben nodded. "I can look through the old footage and see if I get some ideas."

He turned toward the door, and Juniper dashed away.

Sadie and Ben were going to do a big stunt for the final scene. Something spectacular. If she could do that stunt well, she'd show them she was the best.

She just had to figure out how.

Chapter 6
A Plan

At dinner that night, Juniper was quiet, but there was plenty of talk from her parents, so no one noticed her silence.

"Paramount wants to use Lucky in a movie they're shooting," her dad announced as her mother piled macaroni and cheese on Rose's plate.

"That's wonderful," her mom said. "How long's the shoot?"

For the rest of the meal, her parents and Rose

talked about the movie and what their horse Lucky would be doing. While they were busy celebrating, Juniper ate her mac and cheese, deep in thought.

She knew Lucky would be just fine in the movie. The horse had starred in lots of productions, and she was already the best.

Juniper was worried about herself. She needed to think up a way to get herself assigned to the big stunt Sadie and Ben were planning. Then Juniper would show everyone she was the best.

"I've got some homework to do," Juniper said, getting up from the table.

"Okay, honey." Her mom glanced at her, then quickly back at Juniper's dad. "Do they need a lot of horses? Maybe Hercules will be good for the movie."

Juniper hurried into the kitchen, deposited her bowl into the dishwasher, then peered into the dining room. Rose was no longer sitting at the table, but their parents were still sharing ideas about the new movie deal.

Instead of heading upstairs to her room, Juniper grabbed an apple from the fruit bowl and turned toward the back door. She had someone else she wanted to see. She pressed on the doorknob as she turned it so it wouldn't squeak, then she crept outside. After the lock clicked quietly back into place, Juniper ran across the grass to the stables.

Able was munching on some hay and looked up when Juniper burst in. He nickered, nodding his head as though he was letting her know he was glad to see her.

"I missed you, Able," Juniper said, wrapping her arms around his neck. "I love my family, but sometimes I wish I could sleep out here with you. When I'm here, it feels like I don't have any more worries because you'll take them all away."

Able rubbed his head on Juniper's shoulder as if he were telling her he's got her back. "Thanks, Able. I'm so happy we're on *Castle McAvoy* together. It wouldn't be nearly as much fun without you." She sighed. "But, I wouldn't even be on the show if it wasn't for you. You're doing so great. You look beautiful on the set."

Juniper pulled the apple from her pocket and held it out. Able snorted, making Juniper smile. He always snorted when he was happy, and she knew apples made him happy. "You deserve it," she said, as Able bit into the bright green fruit.

"I just wish I looked as good as you on set," Juniper said. "I'm so worried about letting everyone down. Especially Rose. Have you seen how happy she is that I'm on *Castle McAvoy*? She's always happy for me, but now . . . I don't know, it's like it's the best thing that has happened to her in a long time, too. I don't want to mess that up."

Suddenly Juniper heard the scrape of the door on the ground and jumped. Her parents would tell her to go back in and she wasn't ready yet. But when she turned around, it wasn't her parents. "Rose?"

Her sister grinned. "I figured this was where you'd escaped to."

Juniper clamped her mouth shut. Rose hadn't sneaked out to the stables for a long time. She usually left dinner to figure out what to wear to school the next day. Juniper hadn't expected her sister to come here. Had she heard what Juniper just said?

Rose ran up to Juniper and Able and gave her sister a hug. "I'm so proud of you."

"You are?"

"Of course! And you, too, Able." Rose rubbed the horse's nose.

A blossom grew inside Juniper's heart. If her

sister had heard her talking to Able, she must not have minded. "Able's so great on the show, Rose. I can't wait for you to see him."

Rose stroked Able's mane. "I always knew he was going to be special. Just like I always knew you were going to be a great rider. I'm so excited you're on the show. We should have a premiere party. I want all my friends to see you."

"You won't even be able to know it's me. I'll look like the characters."

"I'll know." Rose smiled big, but Juniper sighed.

"I'm afraid they're going to tell me they don't need me anymore. Ever since I did that one stunt on camera, I've been messing up." Juniper cast her eyes downward. "They haven't given me any more stunts. They've just got me rehearsing basic tricks and keeping Able and the other horses fresh."

She glanced up at her sister, hoping for

reassurance, but Rose looked worried, too. "No, they have to keep you on the show. Kim said I—"

"What?"

Rose shook her head. "Nothing. You've worked so hard. They can't take it away from you now."

"I had one idea," Juniper said, "but I don't know how to do it."

"What is it?" Rose asked. "Maybe I can help."

Juniper worried her lip. "Well, they want to do a really big, really spectacular stunt for when Lady Penelope rescues Sir Gregor."

"She's going to rescue him?" Rose's eyes grew wide. "I knew that was going to happen."

"That's not the point." Juniper huffed. "And don't tell anyone. It'll ruin the show."

Rose drew an *X* over her chest. "So, what about the stunt? Will you be doing it?"

"That's the thing. Leigh does all the big stunts and

the Lady Penelope scenes. But if I could show them that I could do it as well as Leigh, they wouldn't be able to get rid of me. Right? I just don't know how."

Rose narrowed her eyes the same way she always did when she was thinking, then said, "How about you suggest a stunt? The most amazing stunt they could possibly have on the show. And it'll be something only you can do. If you suggest it and they love it, which I know they will, they have to let you do it."

"You think so?"

"Of course!"

Able shifted in his stall, then rubbed his head on Juniper's shoulder like he was trying to get her attention.

"Not now, Able. This is important," Juniper said, pushing his nose away. She turned back to her sister. "But what can I suggest?"

"I don't know yet, but we'll figure it out. I know—let's look at movie stunt clips and trick videos for ideas. It'll be just like we used to do before—"

Rose didn't finish her sentence, but Juniper thought she knew what her sister meant to say: before Rose turned fourteen and went to high school. Before Rose started caring more about her friends and what she wore. Before Rose stopped hanging out with her sister. But Juniper left it all unsaid. At that moment, she was just happy to have her sister back.

Juniper hugged Rose and whispered, "I've missed you."

"I missed you, too, Junie," Rose replied. "Let's go find you a stunt. Night, Able."

"Sleep tight, Able," Juniper said, smiling big. "Tomorrow will be special. I can feel it."

It wasn't long before the sisters were lying

on Juniper's bed, watching video after video for inspiration. They looked at clips from dressage, trick championships, freestyle competitions, and movies. They made notes, swapped ideas, and finally, long after their parents had told them to stop, they fell asleep, pencils still in their hands.

When their mother woke them the next morning, Juniper jumped out of bed.

"What time is it? Am I late?"

"Calm down, Junebug," her mother said, chuckling. "You're good, but it is time to get up. Rose, the bus will be here soon. Go get ready."

Rose gave her sister a hug. "Good luck today, Junie. They're going to love it." Then she ran out of Juniper's bedroom.

"Who's going to love what?" their mother asked.

Juniper shrugged. "Just something I was working on for the show. Is Dad waiting for me?"

"He has to take Lucky to Paramount today. I'm going to take you and Able to the studio, then I have to go to work." She eyed Juniper carefully. "Are you going to be all right without one of us there today?"

Juniper nodded, the herd in her stomach starting to canter. "Sure, Mom. We'll be fine."

"Good." Her mother kissed her forehead. "We'll leave as soon as you're ready. Make it quick. Oh, and your dad made me promise to tell you: Don't do anything dangerous."

Juniper held back an eye roll. "I won't."

Juniper shut her door behind her mother, then gathered the notes she'd made with Rose the night before.

"I hope they like this," she muttered, then stuffed the papers into her backpack and got ready to be on the set.

Ben and Marcus were at the show's holding

stables when Juniper walked up with Able.

"Morning," she said as cheerfully as she could. The stampede in her stomach was creating a tornado.

"Hey, Juniper. Hey, Able." Marcus rubbed along Able's neck, and the horse nickered in delight. "Other than Zombie, Able's my new favorite horse."

"He's been doing a great job," Ben said. "You, too, Juniper."

"You really think so?" she asked.

"Don't sound so surprised. You've been wowing everyone here."

Ben said it so matter-of-factly, Juniper wondered if she needed the plan. But then she remembered his words and her dad's words about Leigh. She wanted them to say that about her, too.

"Actually, I had some ideas for the big stunt you need," she said, settling Able in his stall.

Ben looked at her quizzically. "What big stunt?"

"Oh, I heard you talking about it to Sadie. I'm sorry if I wasn't supposed to hear."

Ben laughed, deep and loud. "No, no. That's okay. It wasn't really private. I was just surprised. And you've got an idea?"

Juniper nodded quickly, before she could change her mind.

"Great," Ben said. "I always like to hear new ideas. Let's go see what Sadie says."

Ben and Marcus started walking to the set, and Juniper turned to Able. "Did you hear that? I hope they let us do it. Don't you, Able?"

Able shook his head as though he was keeping flies off. Or getting rid of ideas he didn't like. Juniper wasn't sure which, but he had to appreciate this idea. It was hers, and he was her best friend. "It's going to be great, Able," she said. "I promise."

"Juniper!" Ben called back to her. "You coming?"

Juniper did a little hop, unable to hold in any more nervousness or excitement. "Coming!"

She kissed Able on the nose. "I'll be back with the news as soon as I can. I love you, Able."

Then she ran after Ben and Marcus.

They found Sadie at the set, hunched over a folder and scribbling notes.

"Sadie," Ben said, "Juniper here has an idea that might work for that big stunt you want. Go ahead, Juniper."

Sadie looked up from her notes and smiled. "Great. I'm always up for good ideas. Let's hear it."

Juniper took a deep breath. "My sister, Rose, and I were brainstorming last night, and we thought it would look really cool if . . . well, here . . ." She pulled out the diagrams Rose had drawn. "Sir Gregor could be in a prison carriage pulled by four horses, Able being one. I could be Lady Penelope on another horse, ride up, and jump from my horse to Able. While people are shooting arrows at me, I can roll under Able's belly, then come up in the middle of the two horses, and end up right by the carriage. I can push the driver off, take the reins for myself, and drive the carriage away."

She blinked. Ben and Sadie stared at the drawings. Juniper glanced at Marcus for some courage. Leigh and Pablo had walked up behind him and were peering at the drawings, too.

"It reminds me of the old *Stagecoach* stunt Yakima Canutt did back in 1939," Ben said.

"Yes," Juniper said quickly. "We got the idea from that. Plus some other videos and tricks we already knew."

Sadie nodded. "John Wayne was in *Stagecoach*. Yeah, I remember that. Isn't it considered the most dangerous horse stunt ever done?"

"It sure is," Ben said, shaking his head. "This one's not as dangerous, but it still has a lot of risks."

Juniper's heart fell.

"It would look spectacular," Sadie said.

"You could put a small camera on me so you can see the action close up," Juniper said, hope blooming in her tummy.

Sadie turned to Ben. "That stunt was dangerous because it was 1939, but we've got harnesses we can use now, right?"

"We do," Ben said. "I'd prefer to cut it down to two horses instead of four. Maybe even one. That'll be safer."

"We could also film it in stages instead of one long shot, like in *Stagecoach*," Sadie said.

"That would be better," Ben agreed.

Sadie pursed her lips. "If we can make this work,

it will be a stunt that viewers will talk about for years." She gave Juniper a smile. "Good work."

Juniper felt like her heart might explode from happiness.

"All right, we can give it a try," Ben said. "But Juniper's younger. We should have Leigh on this. She's more experienced."

Juniper's heart fell again. Nooooo. That wasn't what she wanted.

Leigh's eyebrows lifted and she stepped around Marcus, shaking her head. "I can't do that."

Juniper suppressed a smile.

"Which part?" Ben said.

"Any of it," Leigh said. "I haven't done that belly trick yet. This would be a big learning curve for me."

"I can do it!" Juniper was so excited, she shouted the words louder than she'd meant to. She swallowed and tried again. "I can. Able and I have been doing the under-the-belly trick for a while."

Ben eyed her carefully. "I'm not sure you'll have the strength to pull yourself into the carriage."

Juniper held her breath, waiting to see if he'd tell her no again. Finally, he said, "But we could put in some hidden steps and handrails so you can get into the carriage more easily. Between that and the harness, you'll be safe."

Juniper grinned. "Perfect."

Sadie closed her folder with a snap. "Great. Let's get that on the schedule."

The herd inside Juniper's stomach felt like it had turned into a fireworks display.

She was going to do the biggest horse stunt of the entire season.

She would show them she was the best.

Chapter 7
The Big Stunt

That night, Juniper and Rose celebrated the best way they knew how: by feeding apple slices to Able and their other horses, then going over the plans for the stunt. Rose was as happy as Juniper that the show was going to do their idea, and Juniper soaked in all her smiles.

"You're going to be a bigger star than Alicia and Caleb and all the other actors," Rose said, laughing as she spun in the entranceway of the stables.

"I just want to be the best stunt rider," said Juniper. "To have Dad and Ben and Marcus and everyone say that I'm as good as Leigh is. Then they can never make me leave the show."

Rose shook her head. "You have nothing to worry about."

Able nudged Juniper's shoulder, and she sat on the ground beside him. "It is a pretty dangerous stunt, though. Don't you think?"

"You can do it. I know you can." Rose smiled. "You are my brilliant sister. Now, what dress do you think they'll make you wear?"

The next day, when Juniper and Able arrived at the studio, she couldn't stop smiling. She was nervous, but nothing could make her sad. Soon, she would be rehearsing the big stunt with Ben, and she was excited to get started.

As her dad helped Able walk off the trailer,

Caleb came running up to them. "Hey, Juniper, I heard about the stunt. It sounds incredible. I can't wait to see you do it."

Juniper beamed. "Thanks."

"What stunt?" her dad asked as Caleb ran to the studio. Juniper bit her lip.

"I got assigned a stunt for an upcoming episode," she said, trying to keep her voice as even as possible.

Her father raised his eyebrows. "Sounds like it's a pretty big deal."

Juniper shrugged. "Just another stunt."

Her dad squeezed her shoulder. "I can't wait to see it. Okay, I'm not going to hang around the set today. The other animal handlers are doing great with Able, and you don't need your old dad cramping your style."

He winked, then took a deep breath. "Listen, Junebug, I'm sorry I didn't trust you more about doing stunts. I just . . ." He rubbed her arm. "I just want you to be safe."

Tears welled in Juniper's eyes, but she blinked them away. "I know, Dad."

"Good. You're doing really great. Your mom and I are both very proud."

Juniper smiled. "Thank you. Of Able, too, right?"

"Of course! He's the other star in the family."

Able nickered.

"All right," Juniper's dad said, "I'm going to check on Lucky at Paramount. If you need anything, you call me, okay? And stay safe."

"Safe," Juniper said at the same time as him, and grinned. "I will."

Her dad laughed and ruffled her hair.

Rehearsal had been scheduled for early that morning. First, Juniper worked with Able, while Ben, Marcus, and Leigh looked on. From Able's back,

Juniper practiced crawling down his side, under his belly, and up his other side over and over. She had wondered if the trick would be different with the English saddles used on the show, but she got used to it quickly. Their audience applauded every time.

Leigh looked especially impressed. "You have to teach me how you do that," she said during a break.

"It's easy," Juniper said, feeling proud that she could help Leigh. "Well, not easy—it takes a lot of practice and concentration, but you can do it."

After lunch, Able got a rest and Juniper practiced safely jumping from the stirrups of Zombie and onto a horse about Able's size. This was harder, and they were just standing still. Juniper knew she'd have to practice a lot to be able to safely land on Able's back while they're galloping.

That night, Juniper was exhausted. "I feel like I've never worked this hard in my life," she told Able when she brushed him. "How about you?"

He nuzzled her with his nose, and she kissed it lightly.

"It's going to be so worth it, though," she said. "You'll see."

But she tried to silence the herd in her tummy. Now that they'd started working on the stunt, Juniper had seen just how much had to be done—and how big the stunt really was. No matter how nervous she felt, Juniper stayed determined to do this stunt perfectly.

The next few weeks continued like this. Every day, Juniper worked hard with Able on different parts of the stunt. While Able was resting, she worked with other horses on other parts of the stunt. When she wasn't working on the stunt, she went to class, and while Mr. Vela tutored them in things like social studies, she'd draw a stick figure doing all the moves she had to do in the stunt.

Every night, Rose snuck into Juniper's room for an update, but Juniper was so tired, she usually fell asleep in the middle of a sentence.

Finally, they were a week away from shooting. Juniper had made a lot of improvement jumping off Zombie and onto Able, pretending she was getting shot at by arrows, then crawling around Able's saddle and under his belly to get to the other side.

The last part of the puzzle for Juniper was perfecting how she had to jump onto the carriage. Ben had had the production team create hidden places for her feet and hands, kind of like a ladder, at the front of the carriage. By itself, it was easy to climb up.

But when Juniper put the climb with all the other actions she had to do, it was difficult. There was so much to remember. The timing had to be perfect.

And even with the harness Ben had created to keep Juniper safe, having the horses and the carriage around her was scary.

During rehearsals, little things started to go wrong. Juniper would put her foot in the wrong place, would get tangled in the reins, or would not be able to get the harness clear of the saddle to allow her to reach the carriage.

The day before the stunt was scheduled to be shot for the episode, Ben shook his head as he watched. Marcus and Leigh stood with him near the set, and both looked worried. The herd in Juniper's tummy was a full-on stampede, her palms were sweaty, and she missed grabbing the reins.

"Sorry!" she shouted. "It's hard to get around this harness. I'll try it again."

"No. Come in, Juniper," Ben said. "You need to take a break."

"I can get it! I just—"

"It's time to stop." Ben walked over to where Juniper was untangling herself from the horses' ropes. "You're young, and you can only work for limited hours at a time. It's the law, kiddo."

"But we're shooting the stunt tomorrow," Juniper pleaded.

"I know." Ben swallowed. "If we need more time, we'll just have to push the schedule."

Push the schedule! Juniper didn't want to be the reason for the show getting behind. But the animal handler was already taking the horses to get water in the stables, and Ben was heading to the studio with Marcus.

"Come on," Leigh told Juniper. "I'll walk you to costume so you can change before class."

Juniper watched Able walking with the animal handler, wishing she could go to the stables, too. She felt like a failure and didn't want to be with anyone except her horse.

"I've had a hard time with stunts before." Leigh shuffled her feet, waiting for Juniper.

Juniper glanced at her, then started the trek to the costuming area. "I feel like I'm letting everyone down." Juniper pinched her eyes closed to keep back the tears that were threatening to roll down her cheeks.

"Oh, I know," Leigh said. "It's horrible. You feel like you're the worst stuntperson in the world."

"I know, right?" Juniper sighed.

"You're going to get it, though," Leigh said, smiling. "This is a really hard stunt, and I know I couldn't do it. But you're so close."

"You think so?"

"For sure. You'll do great tomorrow."

Juniper pressed her lips together. "I hope so."

The rest of the day went by slowly. Juniper barely heard a word Mr. Vela said in their science lesson, or Ben said in training, or her father said when he picked up Juniper and Able that evening. Every time her dad asked her a question, she nodded and answered, "Fine." But she didn't feel fine at all.

Lying in bed that night, she logged on to the Hoofprints Horse Riding Forum. Instead of looking at the funny and inspiring threads she usually loved, she went to the section where riders posted if they needed help.

JuniRidR: I've got a big stunt to do tomorrow, and I haven't been nailing it in rehearsals. What do I do? I don't want to fail.

PonyItUp: I have that problem all the time in rehearsals for a show.

JuniRidR: What do you do?

PonyItUp: When showtime comes, it always falls into place. I'm more focused when all the people are watching and I'm under all those lights. That adrenaline thing, I guess. You'll get it tomorrow.

JuniRidR: I don't know. This is . . .

Juniper didn't know what to write next. She wasn't going to be in a horse-riding show in an arena like PonyItUp was talking about. Could she count on her adrenaline magically making everything in the stunt go right? She deleted what she'd started to type.

Then another message popped up, and Juniper gasped.

CRains#1: You can do it, **JuniRidR**! Believe in yourself. I believe in you.

Claudia Rains had posted on her question. Claudia Rains said she could do the stunt!

Juniper soaked this in. She posted a quick thank-you message, then logged off so that Claudia Rains's message would be the last thought in her head.

The best rider on the forum, the rider with the most championship wins, believed in her.

Juniper just had to believe in herself.

Before she closed her eyes to sleep, she looked over at Able's stable through her bedroom window.

"We'll do great tomorrow, Able. I promise."

The next day, Juniper stayed close to Able until Ben and Sadie were ready to do the big stunt. Finally, Marcus came to the stable to get them.

"They're ready," he said, breathless from running from the set. "You?"

Juniper sucked in a breath. She put her forehead on Able's cheek. "We're going to be the best, Able. Well, you already are, but after this stunt, I will be, too," she whispered. "I love you. I'll protect you."

She kissed his nose and put a big smile on her face. Even though Able didn't nod his head, Juniper could tell he was excited to get to work.

On the set, Able was costumed and hooked up to the carriage. Juniper got on the back of Zombie. Her dress looked like it flowed around her, even though it had been sewn strategically so it wouldn't get in the way of her stunt.

"Silence, please!" the production assistant shouted, and a hush came over the whole set.

Juniper's heart felt like it was in her throat. She thought of PonyItUp's words. Maybe her adrenaline would kick in when she started, and everything would go perfectly. She hoped so. She also thought of Claudia Rains's message. Claudia believed in her.

She had to do the same.

"Everyone ready?" Ben called out.

"Ready," Juniper squeaked, followed by the others in the scene.

"All right," Sadie said. "Action!"

The prison carriage trundled into the location. Caleb as Sir Gregor shouted, "Help! Get me out of here!" from behind the bars.

Juniper galloped Zombie close to Able at the

front of the carriage. From the driver's seat, Pablo shouted for her to stop, just as they'd rehearsed. She breathed in deeply, then pushed off from Zombie, landing on Able's back in the perfect position.

Yes, she thought. PonyItUp and Claudia Rains were right. She could do it.

Pretending arrows were zinging by her head, she swooped around, then climbed down Able's side, holding tightly to the girth under his saddle. Focused, she continued under his belly, then up his other side.

Now Juniper just had to get onto the hidden ladder and climb up to the driver's seat. So far, everything had gone as planned, even better than she'd ever done it in rehearsal.

"We've got this," she told Able as he kept galloping forward.

Juniper put her foot onto the bottom step at

the front of the carriage, the harness keeping her upright. She reached up to grab the handhold, but her sweaty palms slicked off it.

It's the harness! she thought. *It's not getting me close enough.*

Before she could think herself out of it, she unclipped the harness. She dove forward onto the step, grabbing the carriage.

But her palms were still too wet.

Her fingertips grazed the carriage edge but couldn't grab on.

Juniper dropped backward.

"Nooo!"

She twisted to try to reach for the carriage, the girth—anything. But when she couldn't grab hold, her body fell into Able's side, then onto the ground with a thud.

The carriage screeched to a halt.

Able neighed loudly.

Juniper tried to see if he was hurt, but pain rocketed up her arm when she moved.

"AAAHHHH!"

Chapter 8
Broken Plans

"Juniper!"

Juniper began to sob when her dad hurried through the door of her hospital room.

She'd held back her tears when Ben had rushed her to the hospital, when she'd been wheeled inside, and when her arm had been X-rayed. She hadn't even cried when the doctor began putting the cast on. But when Juniper saw her father, all her pain and fears pushed into her heart, and she could no longer stop her tears.

Ben had been holding her good hand, but now he let it go so her father could get close.

"Thank you for bringing her, Ben," Juniper's father said, then turned his attention back to his daughter. "I got here as fast as I could. Your mother's the only assistant on duty at the vet's office, so she'll see us at home, but she's worried about you. We both are. What happened?"

"I messed up," Juniper said. "I thought I could do the stunt better if I took off the harness, but then I fell. How's Able?"

Her father shook his head. "He's got a bruise on his side."

Juniper gasped, then fell into sobs again.

"He's going to be okay. He's at home resting, and he'll be back to normal in a day or two." He squeezed Juniper's hand. "Your broken arm is going to take a lot longer to heal."

Ben cleared his throat. "I've got to get back to the studio. I hope you recover really quickly, Juniper. We'll see you back on the set when you're ready."

Juniper nodded, her lower lip quivering.

"Thanks again, Ben," her father said, then Ben slipped out of the room.

Juniper winced, and her father turned to the doctor. "How much longer will the cast take?"

"It's almost done," the doctor said. "You're doing great, Juniper. Keep holding your arm still."

Juniper tried to obey, tried not to look at her father, but she was worried he was mad at her. He didn't say anything for a long time—just held her good hand and watched the doctor work.

"I'm sorry, Dad," Juniper said finally.

He nodded slowly. "Ben told me you suggested the stunt."

Juniper focused on the floor.

"It sounded impressive," her father said.

Juniper glanced at him. "It was. Rose and I came up with the idea together. It would've been amazing."

"Except that it was too dangerous."

Juniper gulped and looked at the tiles on the floor again.

"You promised, Junebug." Her father sounded so disappointed, and Juniper's heart felt like it was breaking in two. "You promised not to do anything dangerous. You promised to listen to Ben and stay safe."

"I just wanted to be the best." Tears sprang to her eyes again. "I wanted to make sure they liked me."

Her dad sighed. "Do you know why I've always said that the animals are the actors in our family?"

"Because you didn't think we were good enough."

Juniper's voice was small.

"No, no. That's not it at all." Her father gently wiped the tears from her cheeks. "I knew you and Rose could both be great at stunts, especially you, Junebug. You have a way with horses that most riders would love to have."

Juniper frowned. None of this made sense.

"When I was your age," he continued, "I did stunts for movies."

Juniper's eyes widened. "You did? Mom said you did tricks, but I didn't know you did horse stunts for movies, too."

Her father nodded. "Yep. You know Grandpa trained horses, just like I do, and I was messing around on our old horse Charlotte one day when a director saw me and put me in his movie."

"Wow."

"Don't say wow just yet," her father said. "I was

just like you. I saw these other stuntpeople, and I wanted to be the best one, better than all of them. This was before they had all the safety regulations they have now. So one day, the stunt coordinator asked me to do a stunt that was dangerous, and I immediately said yes."

The doctor carefully moved Juniper's arm, checking her cast, but she barely noticed. She was too focused on her father's story.

"What happened?" she asked when he paused.

"The stunt went badly. I fell from the horse and not only broke my leg, but I injured my knee so badly, I still have problems with it today."

"That's why you can't do tricks? Because of that stunt?"

Her father nodded. "Yes, but more than that. It's because I wasn't safe. I wasn't able to do trick riding professionally anymore, so I lost my dreams of being a stunt rider and a champion."

Juniper pressed her lips together. This whole time her father had been trying to stop her from making the same mistake he had, and she had done exactly that. She looked at the cast on her arm, which the doctor was just finishing.

"Will I be able to ride and do tricks again?" she asked the doctor.

He smiled at her. "We'll know more when this has healed, but if you take good care of it from now until the cast is off, I think you should. With one condition."

"What's that?" Juniper was almost afraid to ask.

"You take your father's advice and do them safely from now on."

Juniper grinned. "I can do that."

When they got home, Juniper wanted to visit Able, but her mother was fussing over her too much.

"You need to rest and eat, Junebug," her mother said, tucking her into bed. "I'll bring up a bowl of my minestrone as soon as it's ready and help you eat. Oh, and cookies. I have some chocolate chip ones. I'll bring those, too."

After her mother left, her father came in carrying the small TV from their bedroom. "You can keep this in here for a couple weeks while you're resting," he said, arranging it on the desk in the corner of her room.

"Thanks, Dad."

"Just until you're better, though, so don't get any ideas." He winked.

As he was finishing with the TV, Rose appeared at the bedroom door, peering at Juniper with worried eyes.

"Junie!"

Rose hurried to give her sister a hug, but couldn't

quite figure out how to get around the big cast on her arm.

"I forgot the remote," their father said, heading out. "I'll be back in a minute."

Rose clasped Juniper's good hand. "I'm so sorry you were hurt, Junie."

Juniper shrugged. "It was my fault."

Rose shook her head. "I've been a horrible sister. I should've protected you." Tears glistened in Rose's eyes.

"You weren't there, Rose. You couldn't have protected me."

"I—" Before Rose could finish her sentence, their dad walked back into the room brandishing the TV remote like a sword.

"Got it! Now to find something good for you to watch."

"Everyone hungry?" Juniper's mom returned

carrying a tray with four steaming bowls of soup and four glasses of water. "I thought this once we could eat in the bedroom to make it easier on you, Junie. Can you sit up a little higher?"

Juniper couldn't help smiling at her family, all gathered around her, caring for her, loving her. A swell of gratitude filled her chest, making her feel light enough to float away.

But as her mother handed out bowls and her father switched channels on the television, Juniper wished her best friend was also there. She gazed out at the stables and hoped Able knew she was thinking of him.

And that she was sorry.

Chapter 9
A New Plan

When Juniper woke up the next morning, she couldn't get the show and the big stunt out of her mind. She replayed what happened over and over again. She should have kept the harness on. She should have pushed harder on the step. She should have been better.

Sadness swam around her as she thought of *Castle McAvoy* and all the wonderful times she'd had working on the show. Now, they'd probably never let her do anything for the show again. She'd messed up her one chance to get her dream. She hadn't been perfect. She hadn't been the best.

Juniper sniffed back tears and thought of Claudia Rains. She always did everything perfectly. How was she so good when Juniper messed up all the time?

The only way to find out was to ask her.

Maneuvering carefully, Juniper pulled her laptop onto her bed and opened it with one hand. She'd had a broken arm for only one day, and it already felt tiresome. Luckily, Claudia Rains's thread on the Hoofprints forum was still on the screen.

Juniper scanned every comment on Claudia's latest post. They were all happy and congratulatory. Juniper didn't feel right putting her question there. Claudia had commented on Juniper's post. Had said she believed in her. Maybe she wouldn't mind if

Juniper messaged her directly.

Opening a chat window, she slowly typed her question with her one good hand:

Hi Claudia, This is Juniper, **JuniRidR**. I just tried to do a difficult trick and failed it big-time. I don't know why I can't get it perfect, like you always do. How do you always get your tricks so perfect? I want to be like you. Thank you for helping.

She took a deep breath, then hit send.

Juniper lay back on her pillow, sure that she wouldn't get a response for a while, if at all. But to her surprise, the three little dots that showed the other person was typing popped up. Juniper watched them, waiting. Was Claudia Rains right there? On her computer? Typing her back?

Bing!

Claudia's reply appeared beneath Juniper's message:

Hi Juniper! I remember you posting about having difficulties. I'm sorry you couldn't get it to work. But that's okay! Honestly, your message made me laugh out loud, because I feel like I never get a trick perfect, and I'm really lucky when I'm able to do it well in competition time, when it really counts. For every video of me doing a trick right, I have hundreds of videos where I messed it up. And if you count all the hours I worked on the trick before I tried to record it, you'd think this was all I ever do—which is pretty much true. But I don't mind messing tricks up and having to do them over and over and over again. Because the best part of being a trick rider is working with my horse, Sahara. She makes all my bumps and bruises worth it. I hope your horse is the same for you.

Juniper exhaled. Claudia Rains wasn't perfect after all. She practiced and messed up just like everyone else.

Juniper thanked Claudia, then read her message again, focusing on one line:

The best part of being a trick rider is working with my horse.

Juniper had been so busy trying to show everyone that she was the best stunt rider, she'd forgotten what she loved doing best—riding around their pasture with Able.

She gazed out her bedroom window at the

stables and hoped he was feeling okay.

Messing up her stunt wasn't the worst thing she'd done. Juniper realized that now. She had put her best friend in danger. She had to make sure she never did that again.

She had to go see Able.

Juniper swung her legs out of bed, but before her toes hit the floor, her bedroom door opened.

"Where do you think you're going, little one?" her mother asked, walking into her room. "You need to rest so you can heal." She smiled big, but Juniper's heart dropped. Her mother would never let her out of the house now.

"How about some pancakes for breakfast? Gotta keep your strength up." Her mother stared at her expectantly.

Juniper shrugged.

"Perfect. I'll bring them right up!" Her mother

disappeared through the doorway but was quickly replaced by her father, asking if she needed anything.

That's right, Juniper thought. *It's Saturday. They're going to fuss over me all day.* She sighed.

Then Rose sauntered into her room, eating an apple.

When her father looked at her sister, Juniper mouthed, "Get me out!" then smiled sweetly when her father turned back to her.

"I don't need anything, Dad," Juniper said.

He started to sit on her bed. "I can keep you company, if you'd like."

"She needs a drink, Dad," Rose said quickly.

Their father nodded and started out of the room. "I can get that."

"You have to help me go see Able," Juniper told her sister when their father had left.

"Mom will kill you if you get out of bed."

"My arm's broken. I'm not sick."

Rose glanced out into the hallway. They could hear their parents busy in the kitchen. The coast was clear. "Come on. I'll take you."

She helped Juniper out of bed then the sisters hurried into the hall and toward the back door when they heard a cough. They both turned. Their father was standing in the doorway to the kitchen, holding a glass of water. Behind him was their mother with a plate stacked high with pancakes. Neither of them looked happy.

"She just wants to see Able," Rose said, her voice pleading. "I'll be with her the whole time and will make sure she's perfectly safe or . . . you can ground me and take away my allowance for the rest of my life."

Their father frowned. "Just so you don't get disappointed later, we're not planning to pay you an allowance for the rest of your life."

"Paul." Their mother pushed past him with the pancakes. "Food first, then you girls can go. But only for a few minutes, and you *must* keep that cast clean. You got it?"

Juniper smiled and nodded. "Thank you!"

She downed her pancakes as quickly as she could. A few minutes later, Rose was opening the door to the stables.

"Able!" Juniper hurried to his stall.

The horse nickered, happy to see her. When she got close, he nuzzled her neck on the opposite side of her broken arm. He knew she had to be careful.

"I've missed you so much," Juniper said, kissing him on his nose. She gazed at his side and saw his bruise. "I'm so sorry, Able. I did this to you. I made this happen. I've been the worst friend."

She wrapped her good arm around his neck.

Rose shuffled her feet. "It wasn't all you, Junie. I was part of it, too."

Juniper looked at her sister. "You just encouraged me to be my best. Nothing wrong with that."

"I knew the stunt was dangerous," Rose said. "I should've been talking you out of it. I'm your sister, and I should've been protecting you. But I didn't. Because . . ."

Juniper leaned on Able. "Because what?"

Rose stepped closer to her sister. "Remember when I told those girls at school that you were on the show?"

Juniper nodded.

"I did it because none of them wanted to be my friend. But when I told them about you, they wanted to hang out with me. So I kept telling them about your show so they'd keep liking me." Rose hung her head.

"But what about Kim? I thought she was your best friend?"

Rose shook her head. "Not this year. She started hanging out with these girls in the fashion club, and they wear nicer clothes than I do and shop together. I don't fit in at all."

Juniper sucked in a breath. That was why Rose had started caring about her outfits more than being with Juniper.

Rose stared at Juniper with sorrowful eyes. "I encouraged you to do that big stunt so those girls would be impressed. But I should've been thinking of you. I'm really sorry."

"I guess we both had our priorities in the wrong place. I wasn't a good friend to Able, either. But we can do better now, right?"

Rose nodded. "Absolutely."

Juniper pulled her sister into a hug with Able.

Chapter 10
A Bigger Stunt

"Surprise!"

Juniper jumped when she rounded the wall of the studio. The stunt cast, Ben, Sadie, and much of the crew and actors were waiting for her and Able at the stables. They'd strung a big "Welcome Back!" banner across the top of the entrance. A table was set out with a cake and cups of punch for the humans, and a bowl of apple slices and carrots for the horses.

Juniper grinned. She had been afraid she'd

never be allowed back on the set, and was excited when, after much begging, her father had said she could go with Able on his first day back.

Marcus brought her a piece of cake that had the G in "Get Well Soon" on the top. "If sugar can heal, your arm should be better in no time with this." He laughed.

"Thanks." Juniper took the cake. "I didn't think you'd want me here since I can't do stunts."

"Of course we do," Marcus said. "You're part of the team."

"They made me promise to text them when you'd be able to come to the set so they could have this party," Juniper's dad said.

"But you made me beg to come back." Juniper pursed her lips at her dad.

"Can't let you get too much of a big head, TV star." Her dad winked. "Of course, the promise you made before I said yes still stands. Nothing . . ."

"Dangerous," Juniper finished. "Believe me, I know!" She pointed to her broken arm.

"All right, I've got to get over to Paramount to help with Lucky. I'll pick you guys up tonight." Juniper's dad patted Able's neck, kissed Juniper on the forehead, then headed back to his truck.

"I'm so glad you're okay—other than your arm, of course," Leigh told Juniper, bringing an apple slice for Able. "I'm sorry you can't do the stunt now. I know it meant a lot to you."

"It did, but . . ." Juniper thought about Able. "I'd be happy to do any stunts, even small ones now. What are they doing for the big stunt?"

"Oh, they're still doing your idea."

"They are?" Juniper was surprised. She had thought that since she wasn't able to do it anymore, they'd try something else. "Who's doing it?"

"Me." Leigh didn't look happy at all, but Juniper couldn't understand why.

"That's great," she said. "Everyone will see even more that you're the best." Juniper meant every word in the best way possible, but she still felt a touch of envy. Even though she couldn't do the stunt and knew the production couldn't wait for her to heal, she still wished she had done it right so that everyone would be impressed.

"I don't care about that," Leigh said. "This was your idea, and you should be doing it. Besides . . ." She leaned in closer to whisper in Juniper's ear. "It's hard for me. And I don't want to break my arm, or worse."

"Okay, everyone!" Sadie shouted over the hum of conversation at the party. "Juniper and Able, we're excited you're back. Juniper, we hope your arm is better really soon. And now, we've got an episode to finish. Leigh, get into your costume. We'll begin shooting as soon as Able's ready on the set."

Leigh nodded. "Will do," she said cheerily, then turned back to Juniper and breathed in deeply. "Cross your fingers for me."

"You can do it," Juniper said, hoping she was right.

The horses, props, and stunt team were assembled on the set within an hour. Juniper sat quietly next to Sadie's director chair. She had to keep telling herself to breathe. She was even more nervous than when *she* had been the one doing the stunt.

All that kept running through her mind was, this stunt was her idea, and if something happened to Leigh, it would be Juniper's fault. When Juniper had suggested it, she had been putting herself in danger, not realizing how it would affect Able. Now

Leigh had been pulled into it, too, and the herd in Juniper's tummy was not happy.

"Action!" Sadie shouted, and the stunt began.

This time, though, it didn't look good from the beginning. Leigh almost missed her jump onto Able, and she was having problems with the crawl under his belly. Able was nervous as well, making him more skittish than usual.

"Hold it!" Ben shouted.

Leigh jumped down from Able, looking relieved. She patted Able reassuringly, but her face still carried a frown.

Juniper hurried over to Able. "You've got this, Able. Leigh is even better than me. She'll do this stunt so well and won't hurt you like I did." Juniper put her forehead on his shoulder. "I'm sorry I got you into this. I'm so sorry. I wish I'd never suggested this stunt now."

Ben had been giving Leigh pointers. Now he walked back to the edge of the set and called out, "Okay, let's go again."

Juniper kissed Able's nose and walked to her seat, but a new idea was running through her mind. If she could come up with an even better stunt, something more spectacular but also much safer, Leigh and Able wouldn't have to do this one.

"Action!" Sadie shouted.

Leigh and Able tried again, but there were still problems, and this time, Leigh slipped from Able's saddle.

"Sorry," she called. "I was off-balance. Can we try again?"

"Wait!" Juniper stood up, then panic quickly ran through her stomach. She hadn't thought of a good enough idea to replace the stunt yet, but she wanted to do something.

"What is it?" Ben asked. "You see something Leigh's doing wrong?"

Juniper shook her head. Her mouth had gone dry, but she had to give them some kind of new idea, something that would be better than this difficult stunt.

"I just . . ." *Think! Think!* She had to think of something.

Everyone on the set was looking at her, waiting. The production assistant glanced at his watch. Juniper was holding up the schedule.

She thought of the research she and Rose had done to come up with this stunt idea, all the different tricks they'd looked at. The most exciting ones had lots of riders doing tricks at the same time, but Juniper and Rose had discarded those because they'd wanted a stunt that would showcase Juniper alone. But maybe that's what they needed now.

"I have an idea for another stunt," Juniper blurted out.

Ben shook his head slowly. "We don't have time to rehearse a new stunt now."

"I know." Juniper had to make them listen. She had gotten Able and Leigh into this, and she had to make it right. "But this stunt will look better and be easier and safer. That's good, isn't it?"

Sadie sighed. "We're not having much luck with this one as it is. Give us your idea, Juniper. We'll see if it'll work."

Juniper gulped. "There are vault competitions with different riders doing tricks over the same horse, and it looks amazing. Instead of Lady Penelope rescuing Sir Gregor on her own, she could get help from some of her ladies-in-waiting. With more people involved in the stunt, viewers will have more things to look at. It'll make it more exciting."

"Hmmm." Sadie narrowed her eyes. "Interesting. Tell me more."

Juniper bit her lip. The herd in her tummy pounded their hooves. "Well . . . like . . ."

"The ladies-in-waiting could be dressed in disguise, so no one knows who the real rescuer is," Marcus said, stepping forward. "I've seen those vault competition videos, too. It's a good idea. One lady-in-waiting could catapult onto Able's back, then onto Zombie's back, next to Able."

"Yes," said Leigh, joining them. "Then another could jump on Zombie then over to Able."

"I could straddle the two horses," Pablo said, "and help Leigh as Lady Penelope get into the driver's seat."

"I don't know. This sounds complicated," Sadie said. "It's not screaming spectacular to me."

"Actually, this could really work," said Anthony,

the man who coordinated the camera shots. "With each camera on one of the actors, and a couple overall shots from different angles, it could look really good."

"What about rehearsal time?" Sadie asked. "Can we fit it into the schedule?"

Ben shrugged. "The moves will look impressive, but the stunts are actually simple, things these guys can do in their sleep. We could probably shoot this afternoon once we can get the blocking in place."

Juniper sucked in a breath. This sounded hopeful.

She stared at Sadie. All eyes were on the director as they waited for her answer. The seconds seemed to drag out into years, until finally Sadie nodded.

"Okay," Sadie said. "Let's break and set up for this."

"Yes." Leigh smiled and turned to Juniper.

"Thank you for thinking of this. You were so brave trying that other stunt, but I didn't want to do it one more time."

"Team stunts are way better than single-person ones, anyway." Juniper grinned.

"Agreed," Marcus said.

"Good job, Juniper," Sadie said, walking over to the group. "You've got a talent for spotting good shots. I know you like the stunt work, but have you ever thought about being a director when you're older? I think you'll make a good one."

"Thanks." Juniper's herd started to gallop in excitement. A director! Juniper had never even thought of it, but it sounded like something she could really like.

She headed over to Able and rubbed his nose. "You'll like this stunt a lot better. And the best part is, you'll still be the star of the show."

Able neighed.

Just like Ben had said, it didn't take long for the kids to get the new stunt to work perfectly. Juniper sat next to Sadie, watching the various camera shots on the screen. It looked even more spectacular than she had imagined.

"You guys were awesome," she said after Sadie had called cut. "I would've applauded, but . . . you know." She pointed to her broken arm, and the stunt kids laughed.

"That's okay," Marcus said. "It felt good. And we couldn't have done it without you."

"Yeah," Leigh said.

"Great job," Ben said, walking up. "Everyone get cleaned up. I need to get these horses to the stables for a rest."

"I'll lead Able," Juniper said.

"Thanks, Juniper. Just be careful of your arm. If

you hurt yourself again, your dad will kill me." Ben laughed.

"Don't worry. I'll be careful." Juniper walked over to Able and gave him a big hug. "You were amazing, boy. The best horse in the whole show."

Chapter 11
Ready to Ride

It was six weeks before Juniper could get her cast off her arm, and by that time, the rest of the episodes of *Castle McAvoy* had wrapped. She was sad that she hadn't been able to perform any more stunts for the show, but she'd had little time to think about it. Inspired by Juniper, Rose had stopped trying to be friends with the popular kids in her class and had gone back to her dream of competing in the trick riding championships, and Juniper was her coach.

"That was a great session," Juniper told Rose as they headed back to the stable. Juniper was riding Able and Rose was on Lucky, fresh off her movie role with Paramount. "Just remember to hold your reins higher."

Rose nodded. "I keep forgetting that. Thanks, coach." She slid off Lucky, then glanced up at Juniper, still on Able's back. "You coming?"

Juniper looked out at the pasture, eyeing the giant elm. That dragon needed some taming.

Juniper shook her head. "Not yet. I want to have some fun with Able for a bit."

The *Castle McAvoy* theme song started playing from within the stables. "That's my phone! Hold on, Able. I'll be right back." Juniper jumped to the ground and raced inside. When she picked up her phone, she saw Leigh's grinning picture. Juniper quickly clicked accept.

"Leigh!"

"Hey, Juniper." Leigh's voice sounded bright and made Juniper miss their days together on the set. "How are you and Able?"

"Great. My arm's all better. We're just about to go out and slay some dragons." She giggled.

Leigh laughed. "I won't keep you, but I just got the start date for practices for the next season of the show. I wanted to see if you'd heard anything yet. Are you coming back?"

Juniper felt a small bit of sadness and envy in her tummy, but she pushed it away. She had enjoyed her time on *Castle McAvoy*, but she really loved her time in the pasture with Able.

"No, I haven't heard anything," she told Leigh. "But it's okay. You and Marcus and Pablo are the best stunt kids I've ever seen. I learned so much from you." And she meant it.

"You're an awesome stunt kid, too," Leigh said, "and an even better friend. You better call me the second you hear, okay?"

Juniper smiled. "I promise."

She clicked off the phone, then headed back out to the pasture. Able neighed as if he was telling her to hurry. He was ready to ride.

Juniper grinned as she climbed up onto his back. "Just you and me this time, Able. Let's go slay some dragons."

When Juniper was ready, Able took off. They raced around the pasture, and Juniper let out a "WHOOO!" Galloping past the dragon tree, Juniper stood up on one stirrup, arms out wide. The wind rushed past her, and she couldn't have been happier.

Back in the saddle, she patted Able's neck. "That was amazing, Able. Want to go again?"

Her horse nodded and they trotted around the

end of the pasture, ready for another run. Claudia Rains had been absolutely right. Doing tricks and stunts was fun, but the part Juniper loved most was being with Able.

"Dragons beware," Juniper cried, a giggle rising up in her throat as Able nickered his own delight.

They got ready to ride, but a shout from the stable stopped them.

"Juniper!" Her dad ran over from their house, waving his phone. "I just got a call from Fay at *Castle McAvoy*."

Juniper climbed down off Able's back. Her tummy roiled. She'd be fine if she didn't get to be on *Castle McAvoy* anymore, but if she was honest with herself, she hoped she and Able could do more stunts together for the show.

"What did she say?" Juniper asked, hugging Able around his neck.

"Something about needing to build up a great stunt team for next season and wanting to have people and horses with the best ideas . . ." He glanced at her.

"Dad! Tell me!"

He grinned. "They want you both back for more stunts next season."

Juniper squealed.

"But you have to promise—"

"Don't do anything dangerous," Juniper echoed. "I promise. Truly. Thanks, Dad."

"You did it all yourself, Junebug," her father said. "I'm proud of you."

"Nope. Not by myself." Juniper kissed Able. "I had the best friend a girl could want with me, right, Able?"

Her horse nodded.

"Okay," Juniper said, "I think I see a troll in the

pasture. You ready to ride, Able?"

Able snorted, and Juniper climbed onto his back.

Soon, they were going to be on their favorite show again. But right now, it was just the two of them, girl and horse, Juniper and Able, riding together.

And Juniper couldn't think of anything better.

Don't Miss These Other

American Horse Tales

Books!

Available Now

November 2021